A CHRISTMAS CAROL

RETOLD BY

Kristina Stephenson

ILLUSTRATED BY

Hoang Giang

PUFFIN

PUFFIN BOOKS

UK | USA | Canada | Ireland | Australia
India | New Zealand | South Africa

Puffin Books is part of the Penguin Random House group of companies
whose addresses can be found at global.penguinrandomhouse.com.

www.penguin.co.uk   www.puffin.co.uk   www.ladybird.co.uk

Penguin
Random House
UK

First published 2020
001

Text copyright © Kristina Stephenson, 2020
Illustrations copyright © Hoang Giang, 2020

The moral right of the author and illustrator has been asserted

Printed in China

A CIP catalogue record for this book is available from the British Library

ISBN: 978-0-241-44939-4

All correspondence to: Puffin Books, Penguin Random House Children's
One Embassy Gardens, 8 Viaduct Gardens, London SW11 7BW

MIX
Paper from
responsible sources
FSC
www.fsc.org
FSC® C018179

THE NAME on the door of the counting house said: *Scrooge and Marley*.
But Jacob Marley was dead; he'd been dead for seven years.

Ebenezer Scrooge – a mumbling, grumbling, mean old miser – ran the
business alone, without a care for anything but his money or a thought for anyone
but himself. Least of all his poor, petrified clerk, Bob Cratchit, who – on this
particular Christmas Eve – was working late . . . as usual.

CHINK,
CHINK,
CHINK!

The sound of Ebenezer Scrooge counting coins drowned out the chattering of Bob Cratchit's teeth as he shivered at his desk.

Outside, a blanket of white topped the houses and carpeted the streets below. Falling flakes of snow and billowing breath filled the air as people bustled about – so much to do, so little time, such Christmas excitement keeping everyone warm.

Not so in the office of *Scrooge and Marley*. There was no warming merriment there, and the fireplace remained as empty as Scrooge's heart.

Until . . .

"Merry Christmas, Uncle Ebenezer!" came a cheery cry as Scrooge's nephew, Fred, burst through the door. "I've come to invite you to dinner tomorrow."

"Bah humbug! What do I care for Christmas?" sniped Scrooge, scowling and shaking a bony finger. "I tell you the same thing every year, Nephew: keep your dinner, keep your festivities, and let me keep myself to myself. Now be gone with you, so I may count my money!"

As Fred left the counting house in a flurry of snow, two gentlemen came in.

"Good evening, sir," said the gentlemen to Scrooge. "We are collecting for the poor and homeless. Might we trouble you for a small donation?"

"You may not!" barked Scrooge bitterly. "There are prisons and workhouses for the poor and the homeless. This money is for ME!"

The gentlemen were horrified and scurried away, leaving a frosty silence in the room, colder than the air outside. It was broken only by the chiming of the clock sounding out the hour.

Time to close the counting house.

"You'll be wanting the day off tomorrow with full pay, I suppose?"
said Scrooge meanly to his clerk. "Be here all the earlier the next morning."

"Yes, sir, thank you, sir, and Merry Christmas, Mr Scrooge,"
said Bob Cratchit cheerily as he hurried out of the door.

Not even children singing carols could melt the icy heart of Ebenezer Scrooge, as snarling, sniping, grimacing and griping he prepared his supper in his house that night. He ate alone as he always did, but when he got ready for bed . . .

"M-M-M-Marley?" said Scrooge, as the eerie figure of his former partner, who'd died on Christmas Eve seven years ago, appeared before his eyes. "What are you doing here?"

"I bring you a warning," replied Marley. "Tonight, you will be visited by three spirits. Listen to what they tell you, Ebenezer, for each of them means to help you."

"S-s-s-spirits?" quivered Scrooge.
"I don't understand."
"You will," said Marley with a knowing smile and, with that, he disappeared.

Scrooge blinked
and rubbed his eyes.
Then, hoping he'd only imagined
Marley, he took himself off to bed.

Scrooge awoke in darkness to the sound of a solemn bell.

DONG!

Ha! No ghosts, thought Scrooge prematurely, as a light, so bright that Scrooge had to squint, flooded his fusty bedchamber.

With a cap on its back, a glowing spirit hovered at the end of the bed. "I am the ghost of Christmas Past," it whispered.

"Long past?" asked Scrooge in puzzlement.

"No, YOUR past, Ebenezer," said the ghost. "Rise and walk with me."

But walk they did not! To Scrooge's very great surprise, the spirit touched his heart, then took his hand and out of the window they . . .

. . . Flew!

It was all Scrooge could do to hold on to his nightcap as they soared through the swirling, whirling snow, far out into the country.

"I recognize this place," cried Ebenezer. "Can anyone see me, Spirit?"

"They cannot," replied the ghost. "These are but visions of a Christmas past."

They came to rest in a cold, dark schoolroom, where a small boy sat hunched and alone in the gloom.

"That's me, as a child," said Scrooge sadly, "forced to stay at school on Christmas Eve."

Just then, a little girl burst into the room and lovingly flung her arms around the boy.

"Father's so much kinder now," she said to the boy. "He says I may bring you home, Ebenezer. Isn't that the most wonderful thing?"

Scrooge's eyes filled with tears, remembering his younger sister, Fan.

"She was always so forgiving," he said. "She died too young, but she had a son – my only nephew, Fred."

"Dry your eyes," said the spirit. "Let's see another Christmas."

the warehouse of his round, jolly, old boss. "He did this every year, you know. Never was there a more generous employer!"

"I see myself again," said Scrooge. "And there's my sweetheart, Belle. We were going to be married, Spirit. Oh, I loved her so."

"Then listen to what they are saying," said the ghost. "Listen well and learn . . ."

"Another idol has taken my place," sobbed Belle to the younger Scrooge. "I cannot marry you, Ebenezer, when all you love is money."

Old Scrooge, who was listening intently, found this memory painful.

"Show me no more, Spirit!" he begged.

But the spirit had other ideas, whisking the miser, in less than a moment, to another place and time. Belle was there – older now, and happy with a husband and child. They were talking about Ebenezer.

"Why, I passed his office tonight, my dear," said Belle's husband. "Quite alone and miserable he was, and on Christmas Eve, too."

Scrooge could bear no more.

"Why do you torment me with memories, Spirit? Stop! Stop!" he shouted, seizing the spirit's cap and forcing it on to its head.

In an instant, the light went out. The Ghost of Christmas Past was gone and Scrooge was back in his bed.

DONG.

Scrooge was woken from a fitful sleep by another solemn bell.

This time no ghost appeared by his bed; only another light, which Scrooge concluded was coming from the next room. Feeling nervous about what he would find there (but very much needing to know), he slid his feet into his slippers and shuffled to the door.

Such a sight met his eyes!

"I am the Ghost of Christmas Present," boomed the jolly spirit. "Touch my robe, Ebenezer. Celebrate with me!"

In the twinkling of an eye, the room dissolved and Scrooge was . . .

. . . out in the street, among the hustle and bustle
and merry commotion of yet another Christmas Eve.
What can I learn from this scene? thought Scrooge,
feeling certain by now that this spirit,
like the first, had a lesson to teach him.

The ghost led Scrooge down a dismal lane, to Bob Cratchit's house – so dingy, so damp, so small, so cramped. Yet here was a family celebrating Christmas full of festive cheer.

Scrooge was wishing he'd paid his clerk more, when he spotted a small, sickly-looking child sitting at the end of the table.

"Who's that, Spirit?" he asked the ghost.

"Tiny Tim, the youngest Cratchit," said the Ghost of Christmas Present.

"But he looks so ill and frail," said Scrooge, unable to hide his worry. "Tell me, Spirit . . . will he live?"

The spirit looked sternly at Scrooge and said, "Only if things change."

The candles burned brightly and the laughter was loud in the house they visited next. Scrooge's nephew, Fred, his wife and a room full of family friends were playing games at their festive table.

Oh my! It looked such fun.

Scrooge joined in, although no one could see him. For these were also just visions. They laughed, they joked, and they poked fun at the miser Scrooge – only Fred raised a glass to his Uncle Ebenezer. "I wish the old man well," he said. "Merry Christmas, dear Uncle Scrooge!"

"Oh, Fred," said Scrooge, "how forgiving you are. You remind me of your mother. To think I turned you away last night. How I wish I hadn't."

The ice in Scrooge's heart was melting as the evening drew to a close.

"Come," said the ghost, "my time on this earth is running out but I have one more thing to show you."

A more dreadful, dismal and desolate place Scrooge had never seen, and oh, what pitiful children, begging in the bitter cold.

"Is there nowhere for these poor children to go?" pleaded Scrooge.

"There are prisons and workhouses," said the ghost, reminding Scrooge of his own cruel words.

"No!" cried Scrooge. "Don't say that. I'm sorry, Spirit, truly I am. I have more than enough money to help these children!"

Somewhere a bell sounded midnight and, with one last look at Ebenezer Scrooge, the spirit disappeared. Alone and shivering in the dark, Scrooge remembered Marley: *three spirits*, he had said.

As the final stroke of midnight faded away, Ebenezer saw it . . .

. . . a hooded phantom coming towards him.

Was *this* the final ghost?

Shaking and quaking, a terrified Scrooge knelt before the spirit. "Are you the Ghost of Christmas Yet to Come?" he asked in a quavering voice. "I fear you more than the others. Show me what you must," he said, "so that I may change my ways."

The spirit pointed to a murky mist where Scrooge saw people talking on yet another Christmas Eve.

"The miserable miser's dead!" said one man.
"Good riddance," said another.
"He had no friends," said a third.
"Nobody will miss him."

"Let's sell his things," said a woman as she bundled up bedlinen and clothes.

"Our debt has gone!" said a couple gleefully. "We will have a happy Christmas."

Everywhere, people seemed glad about the death of a mysterious man.

Everywhere except for Bob Cratchit's house, where sadness filled the air.

Because in Tiny Tim's place at thc table that Christmas there stood . . .

. . . an empty chair.

"Oh, Spirit," said Scrooge, fearing the worst. "Tell me the name
of the man who has died."

The Spirit said nothing, but with a bony finger beckoned Scrooge to follow . . .

. . . through the mist . . .

. . . to a solitary gravestone, upon which a name was carved:

EBENEZER SCROOGE

"No!" cried Scrooge in horror. "DON'T LET THAT MAN BE ME! Don't let it end this way, Spirit. I beg you to give me more time. I can change. I *will* change. From now on, I promise to live my life with kindness, generosity and love. The spirits of the past, the present and the future will stay in my heart forever. Every day will be like Christmas Day, if *only* you will spare me."

The spirit's hand started to tremble on hearing Scrooge's
words and, fearing the ghost was about to leave him,
Ebenezer grasped it. The spirit tried to pull away but
Scrooge would NOT let him go.

"*Please*, Spirit,"
he begged again.
"Tell me I may live."

In the very next moment, to Scrooge's relief, he found himself back in his bedroom. Not holding tight to a ghost at all but to the post of his very own bed.

"I'm alive!" cried Scrooge with so much joy that he almost flew to the window.

He threw open the shutters and let in the light.
Outside, the snow lay crisp and unmarked, and
the frost-covered houses twinkled in the sunlight
with the promise of a brand-new day.

"What is today, my fine
fellow?" called Scrooge, to a
boy in the street below.
"Why, it's Christmas Day,
of course," said the boy.

Scrooge was overjoyed.
"Then I haven't missed it," he said with glee. "I'm the luckiest
man in the world. I've been given a chance to make things better.
I will NOT let the spirits down."

"Do you know the butcher, two streets away?" Scrooge asked the boy. "Is the prize turkey still in the window?"

"The turkey as big as me?" laughed the boy. "Why, it's hanging there now."

"Then run and buy it, you remarkable boy," said Scrooge, tossing him a shilling. "And, if you're back in less than five minutes, I shall give you a crown."

"I'll send the turkey to the Cratchits," chuckled Scrooge gleefully, "but I won't say who it's from. Oh, what a surprise they'll have. Bob, my friend, you and your family shall have a splendid Christmas feast."

Scrooge got dressed in a hurry and ran downstairs to wait.

Soon the boy returned with the turkey. What a size it was! But it was far too heavy to carry to Bob's house.

So, chortling, Scrooge sent it off in a cab while *he* hurried off on his way.

Flakes of snow were falling again, and the streets were filling with people making their way to family and friends. Scrooge, too, was heading somewhere and he didn't want to be late.

He hadn't gone far when, coming towards him, he saw two familiar figures.

Oh my! thought Scrooge with deep regret.
It's the kindly gentlemen who came to my counting house collecting for the poor and the homeless.

"My very dear sirs," said Scrooge warmly, taking them by their hands. "I was mean and selfish to you both last night and I'd like to make amends."

The gentlemen gasped when Scrooge told them how much money he was going to donate.

Could this *really* be the same Mr Scrooge? Goodness! How he'd changed.

A great many people were surprised that day by Ebenezer Scrooge – no longer snarling, sniping, griping, instead skipping down the street, tipping his hat to everyone he passed and wishing them a "Merry Christmas!"

But perhaps it was Scrooge's nephew, Fred, who had the biggest surprise of all.

"Why, bless my soul!" he gasped when he
saw his uncle standing at his front door.
"I've come for dinner, Nephew,"
said Scrooge. "Tell me, am I welcome?"
For just a moment, Scrooge felt sure his
nephew would turn him away.

But Fred flung his arms around Ebenezer.
"You've always been welcome,"
he said. "Come in, *dear* Uncle Ebenezer."
Scrooge thought his heart
would burst with joy.

Bright and early the very next morning,
Scrooge was back in his counting house.

TICK TOCK!

The clock on the wall counted out the time.
Then, nearly twenty minutes late, Bob hurried in through the door.

"What time do you call this?" bellowed Scrooge, pretending to be angry.

"I'm sorry, sir," said Bob, all a-quiver. "I swear it won't happen again."

"Indeed, it will NOT!" said Ebenezer. "Things are going to change!"

With that, Scrooge let out a long, loud laugh and leapt up from his chair.

"I'll start by paying you twice as much and I'll buy you a bigger house," he chortled. "I'll look after you and your family, and I'll find a doctor for Tiny Tim. He WILL get well again, dear Bob, I'll make sure of that. Oh, Bob, my friend, I've behaved so badly but I *promise* to make things better."

And so it was from that day on – Scrooge kept every promise.
To young and old, rich and poor, he showed kindness, generosity and love.
To Tiny Tim, who did get well, he became like a second father.
And, to all the people who'd known him before, he became a better man.
He lived every day with Christmas in his heart, honouring all three spirits.
Scrooge never saw the spirits again, but that was of little matter.

*For they had taught him how to celebrate Christmas
and he would never forget!*